McCordsville Elementary
Media Center

Kogi's Mysterious Journey

ADAPTED BY Elizabeth Partridge

ILLUSTRATED BY Aki Sogabe

DUTTON CHILDREN'S BOOKS • NEW YORK

Immerse yourself in nature,
listen to what nature tries to tell you in its quietness,
that you can learn and grow.
—CHIURA OBATA, TRADITIONAL JAPANESE BRUSH PAINTER

TO MY GODSONS,
STEPHEN SEIICHI AKANA
AND JASON KATZ-BROWN
E.P.

TO MY AUNTIE WHO LOVED CARPS
A.S.

The epigraph on this page is taken from Chiura Obata's 1965 oral history, conducted in Japanese by Masuji Fujii and translated into English by Akiko Shibagaki and Kimi Kodani Hill. The original oral history is part of the Japanese-American Research Project, Department of Special Collections, Young Research Library, UCLA.

CIP Data is available.

Published in the United States by Dutton Children's Books,
a division of Penguin Young Readers Group
345 Hudson Street, New York, New York 10014
www.penguin.com

Designed by Ellen M. Lucaire

Manufactured in China
First Edition
1 2 3 4 5 6 7 8 9 10
ISBN 0-525-47078-6

Every month when the full moon
rises over Japan, people gather on
the shores of Lake Biwa. Fathers
hold children high on their shoulders,
hoping to catch sight of a golden
fish leaping from the water. Mothers
stand close and whisper this story. . . .

Long, long ago, there lived a painter named Kogi. With careful strokes of his bamboo brush, he drew mountains and trees and waterfalls. He painted Lake Biwa, warmed by the summer sun and lit by the winter moon.

But no matter how hard he tried, something was always missing.

Early one spring morning, Kogi took his brushes and rice paper down to the lake. A waking loon called out, and a frog plopped into the water. Kogi watched his friend Basho, the fisherman, pull a thrashing fish into his boat.

Quickly Kogi dipped his brush in ink. With eager strokes, he drew Basho working.

As the boat glided toward shore, Kogi sprang back and studied his painting. Basho looked stiff, and the boat seemed heavy in the water. Kogi threw down his brush in frustration.

Basho's boat scraped on the pebbles as he pulled it to shore. He held up his catch for Kogi to see.

The glistening fish gave Kogi an idea. He asked Basho for a small, silvery-blue one. Its scales shone in the morning light.

Kogi studied the graceful curve of its back, the gleam in its round eye. Then he picked up his brush and painted. But as he worked, the fish's eye clouded over, and its scales dulled.

Kogi looked at his painting and dropped his head into his hands in despair. The fish he had drawn also seemed lifeless and dull.

The next day, Basho chose for Kogi a fish so fresh, it gasped at the empty air and struggled to flip back into the lake. Basho threaded a rope through its gills and handed it to Kogi.

Holding tight to the rope, Kogi hurried home and released the fish into a large tub of water.

He watched as the fish lay on its side. It opened and closed its gills, breathing in the life-giving water. Finally the fish righted itself and swam in tight, nervous circles.

Kogi set aside his brush and rolled up his paper scroll. He knew his painting would capture only the fish's fear and yearning to be free.

Kogi carried the fish back to the lake and waded in. Small waves tugged at his robes. With a murmured prayer of thanks, he lowered the fish into the water. It lay still for a moment, then burst from his hands with a powerful thrust of its tail.

Delight filled Kogi as he felt the joy of its freedom. This was what he wanted to capture in his painting!

Kogi waded farther into the water, looking after the fish with longing.

One more step, another, then suddenly his feet slipped out from under him and he was struggling in the water, unable to breathe.

A tingling shot through Kogi's body. His arms turned into long, flowing fins, and shimmering golden scales covered his body.

Kogi swept his tail from side to side and sped through the water with a freedom he had never imagined. He plunged down into the lake's depths, pushed through weedy forests, and explored huge underwater caverns.

As the sun set, the lake darkened
and lay quiet. Kogi swam slowly
upward. Breaking the surface, he
saw thousands of stars glittering
in the sky.

The moon rose slowly, flooding
the lake with light.

In the vast silence, peacefulness
filled Kogi. His spirit reached out
to touch the stars. He no longer
knew if the stars were in the sky
or if the sky were in him.

The next morning, hunger woke Kogi early. He wriggled through the reeds in the shallows as a brilliant dawn lit up the day. Fishermen pushed their boats into the water, the flat wooden bottoms grating on the pebbles.

The sound terrified Kogi. He knew about fishermen and their sharp hooks! Quickly he fled back to the cool, safe depths of the lake.

Hours later, Kogi swam to the surface. Wind blew the lake into rolling waves. A surge brought the smell of something delicious. As he swam toward it, Kogi saw a baited hook that had been thrown into the water by a fisherman. He almost snapped at the bait, then remembered Basho's catch. With a thrust of his powerful tail, he turned and sped away.

The following day, Kogi nibbled on weeds and caught small insects hovering near the surface.

Again he saw a baited hook and felt his stomach twist with hunger. As he swam closer, he saw that it was Basho's line. Surely his friend wouldn't hurt him! Kogi lunged for the bait. A shock of terror ran through him as Basho tugged on the line, setting the hook deep in Kogi's cheek.

Kogi headed for the deep waters of Lake Biwa. He swam desperately, dragging Basho's heavy boat, the hook tearing at his cheek. Every time he stopped to rest, Basho pulled in the line another few feet.

Suddenly the dark shadow of the boat loomed over him. Basho heaved Kogi out of the water and flung him down in the boat.

"What are you doing, Basho?" Kogi yelled at his friend. "It's me, Kogi!"

Basho heard only the water lapping at the sides of his boat. He wrenched the hook out of Kogi's cheek and threaded a rough rope through his gills.

"You are the biggest, most beautiful fish I have caught in a long time," Basho said. "You will make a fine meal." He dropped Kogi in a basket and rowed quickly back to shore.

Kogi lay gasping for breath in the dry air. The sun beat down on his skin until Kogi thought it would crack into a thousand pieces.

Basho swung Kogi over his shoulder and carried him to a rich man's house. The cook bought him immediately.

He threw Kogi down on the chopping block and grabbed a long, gleaming knife.

"Don't kill me," Kogi cried out.

But the cook heard only the rice, boiling in the pot. With one swift stroke, he sliced deeply into Kogi's flesh.

A searing pain filled Kogi, then there was only blackness.

It was still dark when Kogi felt his firm sleeping mat underneath him. Breathing deeply, he opened his eyes and sat up. He moved his arms and legs in wonder and touched his cheeks. He trembled as once again he felt the hook tearing at his flesh.

For many days Kogi walked with a swaying gait, his body moving from side to side like water weeds pushed back and forth by the waves. When he felt well enough, he took his brushes and rice paper down to Lake Biwa.

For a long time, Kogi sat quietly. He remembered the caverns and weedy forests deep in the lake. He remembered the moonlight washing across the dark water. Most of all, he remembered the freedom he had felt.

Kogi unrolled his paper scroll and picked up his brush. He painted the rugged mountains and the waiting lake. He added reeds swaying in the breeze and a fish leaping in joy from the water. He drew all this and the silence within it.

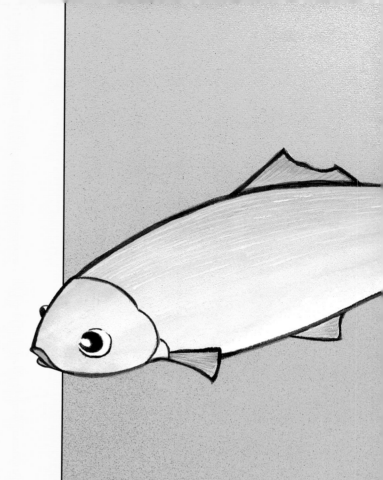

Kogi painted all that day and
then the next. He painted fish after
fish, only surrendering his brush
when the sun set and a sliver
of moon rose over the lake. He
painted every day, until the rising
moon was round and threw silvery
light across the lake.

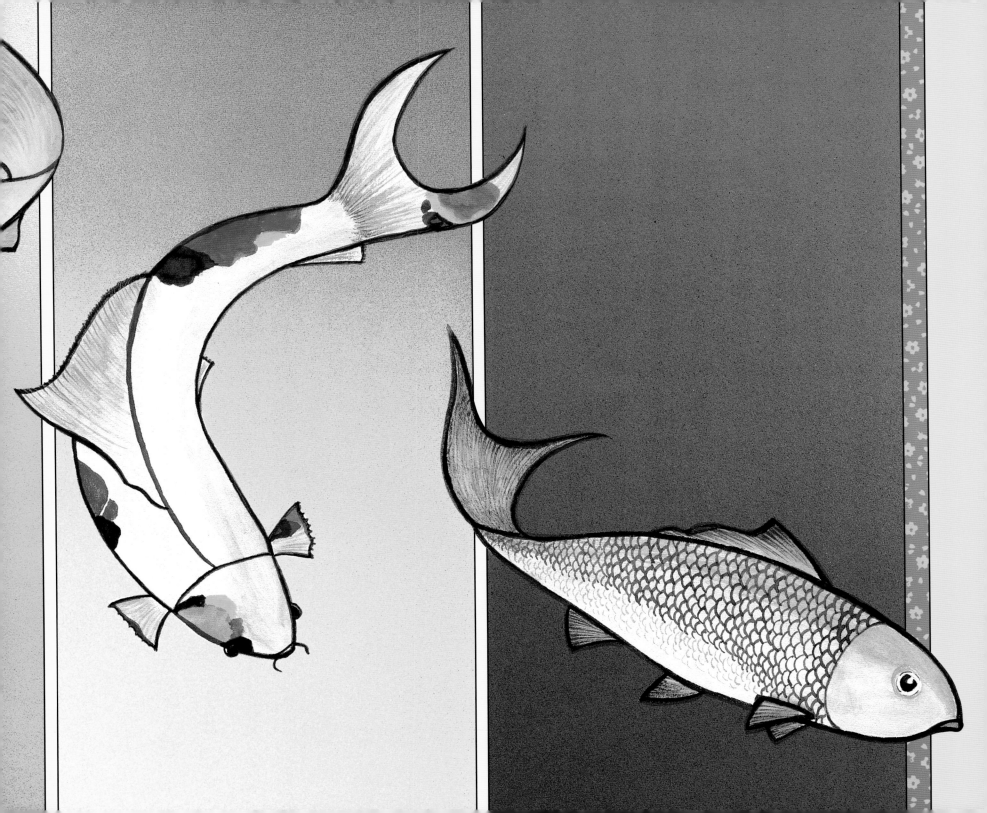

For the last time, Kogi put down his brush. He gathered up all his fish paintings and carried them to the edge of the lake. Wading into the water, he unrolled the scrolls.

One by one, the fish wriggled off the paper and swam away.

Kogi stepped deeper into the water, looking after the fish with longing. One more step, another, then suddenly he was swimming, his powerful golden tail sweeping from side to side in the silence of Lake Biwa.

That was many years ago.
And still people come every
month when the moon is full,
hoping to catch a glimpse of a
golden fish leaping in the waves.

Afterword

Several years ago I wrote a picture book, *Oranges on Golden Mountain*, the story of a Chinese boy who comes to America in the late 1800s. Aki Sogabe, who is Japanese-American, illustrated the book with exquisite paper cutouts. Delighted by Aki's artwork, I wanted to write another story for her to illustrate. I especially loved the fluidity and movement in her images of water and fish, and I turned to Japanese folk tales for inspiration.

A Buddhist priest-painter named Kogi jumped out at me from the pages of a book called *Tales of Moonlight and Rain,* by Akinari Uyeda, translated by Kenji Hamada. I found that Kogi had been fascinating people for a long time. His story was first written down in tenth-century Japan. Kogi is said to have been a real man who lived in the ninth century, drawing many things. It's claimed that some of his paintings still exist—except for the fish, which all swam away.

Kogi continues to captivate Americans as well as the Japanese. Other English adaptations of his story have been included in Lafcadio Hearn's *The Boy Who Drew Cats* and Rafe Martin's *Mysterious Tales of Japan.* These twentieth-century versions emphasize the supernatural aspect of Kogi's journey. While I loved the magical way Kogi turned into a fish, I was even more fascinated with his mysterious, wonderful journey as an artist.

Traditionally, Japanese painters are taught to seek inspiration in nature, and to capture the spirit of a subject, rather than just its physical form. They are urged to deeply understand, to *become,* what they are painting. They learn to be patient, and to use the brush with both vitality and restraint.

My thanks to Kogi and the many people who have kept his story alive, allowing me to share it once again.

—ELIZABETH PARTRIDGE